Luke's First Adventure

K Harper

DEDICATION

Dedicated to my brother, gone but never forgotten.

Luke's First Adventure

Part of the series: Five Worlds Apart

Written by K Harper

Luke's First Adventure

Eight years had passed since Luke first displayed his unusual bouts of strength. He now stood a tall, slim build 10-year-old who attended St Mark's; a local two-form entry, state-run school in Highgate. Luke was popular and belonged to a large friendship circle, other children seemed to gravitate towards him and Luke liked this, for the most part. Things were not always so great for Luke at school and his mother, Sylvia, went through many ordeals in the earlier years of his schooling. She often found herself having to fight against the school governors and what was then the old Head-Teacher, to keep Luke from being permanently excluded. This wasn't easy as Luke exhibited extreme episodes of anger when he was younger, which would often surface and then erupt uncontrollably, whilst he was at school. Unfortunately, on occasion, his anger would result in broken classroom furniture and fittings. During a particular incident, his maths teacher Mr Humphreys wound up with a broken arm. This was a result of Mr Humphreys trying to pull Luke off another child, that he had pinned down on the floor. Regrettably, in Luke's fit of rage, he struck out with his arm in response to feeling a hand on his shoulder, which unbeknownst to Luke was Mr Humphreys in his attempt to intervene. The sheer power in Luke's very effortless, knee-jerk-arm-movement resulted in Mr Humphreys being thrown back onto one of the tables where he then landed with a crack, onto his elbow. Luckily for Luke, his maths teacher had a soft spot for him and he was another person, just like Sylvia, who pleaded on Luke's behalf, to the Head-Teacher for him to remain at school.

At the time, Sylvia and Grant were desperate and out of ideas, until they were introduced through a friend to a therapist called Dr A. Ashworth. Prior to meeting Dr Ashworth, they had sought help from behaviour specialists, therapists and a new mindfulness coach in the local area. Despite the recommendations and their relentless efforts, no one seemed to know what to do. Dr Ashworth seemed to work his magic on Luke and within 6 months of regular weekly sessions he seemed a different child. A child that now had control over his emotions and a purpose behind his eyes. Luke never talked to his parents about what he and his therapist Dr Ashworth covered in their sessions, which at first was hard for Luke's parents as they wanted to be a part of the process in order to support him. Nonetheless, Sylvia and Grant told themselves that a "happier Luke was a better Luke."

Luke had made it to the final term of school, he was in year 6 and had been accepted to his first choice of secondary school, Highgate Hill. He was excelling in English and maths and he had managed to remain focused and calm. And to Sylvia's relief, other parents were starting to invite Luke to birthday parties again. Although every once in a while a flash of his old temper would surface, which tended to be when a close friend of his was being bullied by someone bigger. Luke was loyal to his friends and was always ready to jump in to defend them if he felt an injustice was taking place. Fortunately, the other children were aware of Luke and remembered from previous years how strong he could be. This meant that Luke's anger and strength were to everyone's relief, kept at bay throughout his last year of school.

The summer holidays were fast approaching and both Luke and his parents were looking forward to spending their time in Centre Peaks. This had become a yearly tradition for Luke's family, made possible ever since Sylvia had passed her law degree; and Grant, Luke's father, had some years back progressed from supervisor to warehouse manager. This meant his hours were more flexible, he could set his own holiday time, and most importantly, he did not have to work the night shift anymore. They were all looking forward to the summer holiday. His parents were also nervously excited about the September that would follow, when they would have the joyous occasion of seeing their 'not so little boy', go off to secondary school, at Highgate Hill.

It was the end of the week, Luke was wrapping up another Friday at school and he was rather excited. He had plans to stay at his cousin Mark's house in Bermondsey, South London. Luke and Mark had always got on exceptionally well and had a very special relationship, as cousins often do. They were both only children and saw each other more like brothers and they would only have to look at each other before they would end up in fits of uncontrollable laughter. This laughter would sometimes get them both into a little bit of trouble at the dinner table, where on occasion, they would be asked to leave the table until they could control themselves. Mark was a year and a half older than Luke, although they had so much in common that the age difference was not a factor in their relationship. Mark was also shorter and slighter in stature. It had been a while since they had last seen each other and Luke could hardly contain his excitement as he sat at the back of the car heading towards Bermondsey.

Luke's mum was also looking forward to catching up with her sister.

"Luke did you remember to pack your toothbrush and your flannel?" asked his mum as she looked at Luke in the rear-view mirror.

"Yes mum," sighed Luke "and my socks and my pants."

Sylvia smiled to herself.

"Now make sure you are on your best behaviour Luke, I don't want to pick you up in the morning and have to hear that you haven't been doing 'good listening' to your auntie."

Luke stayed quiet in his seat and rolled his eyes as he looked out of the window to see the River Thames on his left-hand side.

"Look we're nearly there," said Luke as a big, broad grin began to develop on his face as they neared Mark's house.

As the car slowed just outside the house, they could see the curtain moving and peeking out from the side was Mark. He too bore a grin that was just as broad and contained an equal level of excitement as Luke's. He was waving at them jumping up and down.

"Sylvia," cried Janice.

"Janice," laughed Sylvia as they embraced each other in a hug.

"Come in come in," said Janice.

"Aunty J," said Luke, as he too hugged her.

"But wait, look how much the boy has grown," said Aunty Janice in a patois dialect.

They all laughed, the boys looked at each other and grinned and then ran off to Mark's bedroom to play.

Sylvia and her sister spent their time catching up over a cup of tea as the boys played upstairs.

"Right, I had better be off sis," said Sylvia as she made her way to the kitchen door.

"Luke, I'm going now, come down here and give your mother a hug please."

The boys came crashing down the stairs.

"Bye mum," said Luke, as he gave her a

quick hug and ran back upstairs.

"Bye auntie," said Mark, as he too chased Luke in hot pursuit towards the direction of his bedroom.

"See you tomorrow," Sylvia called out up the stairs.

"See you tomorrow sis," said Janice.

An hour had passed since Luke's mum had left, and the boys had been playing a game online on the PS3 and were beginning to feel hungry.

"Mum!" yelled Mark from his bedroom door, "we're hungry, when's lunch?"

Mark yelled again and still didn't receive a reply.

"Maybe she can't hear you?" suggested Luke.

Mark sighed, "Wait here, I'll go and find her."

"I'll come with you," said Luke as he threw his controller on the bed and they both ran downstairs to find Mark's mum.

"There you are!" said Mark. "Could you not hear me calling you mum?"

Mark's mum was sat at the kitchen table and smiled as she looked up at the boys from an article she was reading on her tablet.

"Now you know I don't reply to anyone who shouts at me from the top of the stairs Mark, if you have something to tell me you can come and find me."

Luke sneakily poked Mark and tried to contain his laughter by attempting to hide his face by looking down at the floor.

"The same goes for you too young man, I'm sure your mother tells you the same thing."

Mark gave Luke a look that said, ha-ha she got you too, then they both fell about laughing as usual.

"Now what was it you boys wanted?" asked Janice.

Moments later the boys were sat at the kitchen table, busy, tucked into ham and cheese sandwiches, with crisps on the side that Janice had prepared for them.

"Now boys, I need a few things from the shops this afternoon if you wouldn't mind picking them up for me."

"Sure mum," replied Mark.

"And I suggest that you take yourselves to the park up the road before you go to the shops. Play some football or something, you have played plenty enough on that PlayStation thing."

Luke sat and thought to himself, 'wow we're getting to go the shops, by ourselves, mum never sends me to the shops on my own.'

He then began to think about all the fun they would have at the park and whether it had a cool climbing frame. He could hear Mark's mum talking in the background as he was daydreaming, the last thing he heard her say was, "I'm off for a midday nap, make sure you are both back by 4 pm at the latest for dinner!"

Both Luke and Mark had finished eating and couldn't wait to get to the park.

"Okay," they both chimed together, as they raced upstairs to retrieve Mark's football.

The boys being typical ten-year-olds decided to go to the shops first, against the advice of Mark's mother. The local park was a 10-minute walk from Mark's house, whereas the shop was just 5; and they wanted to be able to get the boring shopping part out of the way first. The boys laughed and raced each other down the street, along the old Victorian terraced houses, practicing their passing skills with the football as they went. Once or twice the ball rolled out into the road, much to the annoyance of the passers-by and motorists, who were either having to move quickly to one side or had to stop their cars abruptly as they were driving. Once they were at the shops, they quickly set about trying to fill the shopping basket as speedily as they could, with items from the list Mark's mum had left them.

"Crisps?"

"Check!" shouted Luke from the other aisle.

"Bread?"

"Check."

"Milk?"

The list went on until both boys met at the front of the shop with their baskets filled with the items from Aunty J's list.

"Hello Mark," said the man behind the counter, "are you helping your mother today?"

"Yes," said Mark "and I brought my cousin Luke with me, he's staying with us this weekend."

Luke smiled at the shopkeeper and stayed quiet.

"Oh very nice," said the shopkeeper as they paid with the money Janice had left them.

"Have you boys seen this?" said Mr Sunil as he pointed to his laptop just beyond the counter.

Luke and Mark looked at the screen.

"Wow they've really gone and done it!" exclaimed Mark, who Luke noticed was bubbling over with excitement.

"Cool huh?" said Mr Sunil.

"Man, I want to get me one of those!" said Mark, referring excitedly to one of the little robots shown on the screen, that was advertising its ability to carry washing from one room of the house to another.

Mark continued, "Then I wouldn't have to do the shopping for mum, I could just send the robot out."

Mr Sunil and Luke laughed.

Luke recognised the man shown talking on the screen, who was explaining the primary function of the robots.

"That's Robert Mann isn't it?"

"Yeah," replied Mark. "He's super cool! You know he was the first person to introduce facetime on phones."

Luke recalled his father talking about Robert Mann a few years ago and remembered him saying that he wasn't such a great person, something about creating a workplace that was overly reliant on machinery.

Luke felt a nudge in his side, it was Mark.

"Come on, let's go and play football."

"Make sure you are both good boys, stay

out of trouble okay."

"Yes Mr Sunil," said Mark as they made their way out of the shop.

Whilst they walked up the road towards the park, Luke began to think, 'I don't know any of the shopkeepers by their name where I live and they certainly don't know my name. Maybe I should tell my mum that I want to go the shops on my own.'

The boys had finally reached the park and could hardly contain their excitement as they neared the football pitch. As they opened the rusty metal gates, they spotted a group of boys playing 'keepie uppie' at the far side of the pitch and so, decided that they would play at the other end. They rushed over to the goalposts, dropped the bag of shopping and began to take turns playing keeper and striker. They were having a whale of a time in the park and almost didn't notice when two of the boys from the group that had been playing at the other end of the pitch approached them.

"Do you lot wanna play two on two?" asked the taller of the two.

Luke and Mark looked at each other, Luke shot Mark a look as if to say, 'no, we don't know them.'

Mark had obviously not picked up on this and said, "Yeah sure! What are the teams?"

"Us two versus you guys," said the shorter one this time.

Luke thought that they looked a good year or two older than him and Mark and something struck him as odd about them. He just couldn't quite put his finger on what it was yet.

"Our mate Paul, over there, can be the keeper," continued the shorter of the two boys.

Luke noticed that they had very grubby hands and that their trainers were quite worn, especially the shorter kid's trainers which had visible holes at the sides. The taller of the two had a shaved head and a gold studded earring that stuck out of his left ear. Luke thought to himself that it was usually only the naughty boys in school that had their ears pierced. Nonetheless, the boys seemed quite friendly and as they began to play Luke started to loosen up. It was a very tense and close game,

1 nil to Luke and his cousin, 1 all, 2-1 to the challengers, 2-2, 3-2 to Luke and Mark and so on. They had been playing for at least twenty minutes and it was down to the final point, winner takes all.

The boy with the shaved head had started to become very physical with his challenges and his friend with the holes in his trainers had started to pull at Mark's t-shirt, in his attempt to keep pace with him, every time he won a challenge.

"Get off!" shouted Mark as he whizzed past the boy defending him.

He passed to Luke and "GOAAAAL!" shouted

Mark.

Luke and Mark grinned at each other and celebrated with a high five.

"You guys cheated," said a voice from behind them.

"Yeah right," Mark said as he laughed in disbelief. "Says the biggest foulers in the south," he continued.

Luke laughed, the boys didn't like the comment, or the laughter coming from Luke and his cousin. They continued to scowl at them.

"You're just lucky my leg was hurting today," exclaimed the taller of the two.

Luke and Mark looked at each other and rolled their eyes, they decided it was best to not taunt the two strangers anymore.

"Catch you next time," said the shorter boy as he barged past Mark. "Come on Paul, let's go."

The three boys headed towards the gate, Luke and Mark talked about the game as they played keepie-uppie.

"Did you see the way I crossed you that ball? You saw how I twisted up that little one right?"

Elated with their win the conversation continued in the same vein until Luke looked at his watch.

"Mark, it's ten to four, didn't your mum say we needed to be back by four?"

Mark looked at Luke.

"Uh oh, we had better be quick," he said and proceeded to scoop up the football. "Get the bag Luke," said Mark.

Luke turned around to face the goal where they had left the bag of shopping.

"It's not there!" he cried.

"What!" exclaimed Mark.

"It doesn't make any sense, I remember putting it right there, just behind the left post of the goal," said Luke.

Mark wasn't listening, he was looking across

the pitch and out into the distance in the direction of the boys who had just left.

"Hold on a minute," said Mark. "Their mate Paul, look, what's that in his hands?"

Luke squinted his eyes and could just make out a plastic bag.

"That's our bag!" cried both boys in unison.

"Quick let's catch them up," stressed Mark, as he began to make pace towards the gates.

The three boys were nearing the edge of the park, close to the fence that led to one of the entrances onto the street. Luke and Mark set off after them sprinting at full speed now.

"Oi," shouted Mark as they drew closer to the boys.

The trio stopped in their tracks and turned around with a smile on their faces that said, 'took you long enough.'

"What do you want?" sneered the tallest boy, with the intimidating shaved head.

"That's our shopping bag, give that back!" snapped Mark.

Luke remained quiet, his fist was clenched and his eyes narrowed in fight mode.

"It's our bag now!" shouted the shorter one.

"Yeah come and get it if you dare," sneered the taller boy.

Paul dangled the bag around laughing. "They're too scared," he said mockingly.

This time it was Luke's turn to speak, "Give that bag back now! or you will regret it."

"Yeah that's right," said Mark, taking a step forward to confront the boys further.

Smack! Suddenly Mark fell to the ground, his face held by his hands. The tallest of the boys had punched him straight in the cheek. Luke could no longer contain the rage that had been building in him and without warning he raced towards the perpetrator, lifted him by his legs and threw him clean over his shoulders, at least four feet in the air and onto the grass, where he landed with a crack!

"Aaagh!" the boy cried out, "my leg, my leg."

Luke didn't stop there, he proceeded to make his way over to the boy with the very worn trainers. The boy tried to take a swing at him as he neared, Luke caught his fist just inches from his face and grabbed hold of the boy's wrist with both of his hands. From the floor where he still lay, Mark watched on, mesmerised as Luke started to swing the boy around in circles, like an Olympic hammer. The boy went flying as Luke released him, this time, at least five metres away and landed with a thud onto the grass. Luke was out of control, he felt hot and tense and began to make his way towards the third boy, Paul, who was clearly not the fighting type.

"Please not me, it wasn't my idea. Here, have your shopping bag," he cried, as he hastily backed away.

Unbeknownst to Luke, the commotion in the park had drawn quite the audience of onlookers from passers-by. A woman who stood just outside the park, next to the fencing, called out, "Young man stop! I've called the police, they are on their way."

Luke continued after the boy.

"Luke, Luke STOP!"

Luke felt a familiar grip on his shoulders, it was his cousin Mark. He was up, albeit a little dazed; and his cheek noticeably swollen, nonetheless, he was able to hold Luke back. Luke finally calmed down and managed to snap out of his rage.

"We've got to go Luke, that woman has called the police, we are going to be in trouble. My mum is going to kill us."

The growing sound of sirens could be heard in the background as the boys made their way out of the park, and they could see lights from the police car pulling around the corner. Mark spotted a friendly face beckoning them over, it was Mr Sunil from the newsagents.

"Boys quickly, come in here," he called.

The boys ran over to the shop.

"Hurry," beckoned Mr Sunil.

Mr Sunil closed the door behind them as they entered the shop and then proceeded to turn over the open sign, to say closed.

"You'll be safe here for a minute, I'll talk to the police, you don't say anything, you understand?"

They both nodded and were quiet. They had been through a whirlwind of emotions over the last ten minutes and were exhausted; and visibly upset. Mark couldn't help but stare at Luke, he wasn't sure what he had just witnessed. Looking out from the shop window, Mr Sunil could see the police car parked across the road and the woman who had called them. She was talking to the police officers, who stood taking notes next to their car. She pointed over in the direction of the park whilst she spoke, and then she pointed directly at the newsagents.

The boys jumped as they heard a loud knock on the door.

Mr Sunil slowly opened the door, "Yes officers, how may I help you?"

The female police officer spoke, "We have reason to believe that two boys who were involved in an altercation in the park just moments ago are seeking refuge in here. Is that correct?" she asked.

"It might be," said Mr Sunil warily.

"Are you the registered owner of this shop sir?"

"Yes I am," said Mr Sunil, "and I have known one of these boys a very long time, he's a very good boy, they both are, I don't want them to be in any trouble."

"Well if you would let us come in and maybe we could have a chat with them, get their side of the story," said the male officer.

"Okay just talking," said Mr Sunil firmly.

"Thank you," said the officers.

Mr Sunil called the boys out from where they were hidden behind the counter, looking petrified, they slowly emerged.

"It's okay," said the female officer reassuringly. "The women from across the road said you were involved in a fight."

The boys nodded.

"Listen, I saw everything, those hooligans hit Mark first, here, look at his cheek," said Mr Sunil.

"That looks a bit painful, are you okay? Mark isn't it?" she asked, as she jotted down his name into her book.

"Hold on, shouldn't their parents be here if you are going to speak to them?" interrupted Mr Sunil.

"Well we are just having an informal conversation at the moment Mr Sunil," asserted the male officer, "but yes it might be a good idea to call their parents down here."

Mark quickly interjected, "this is my cousin Luke, he doesn't live here, he's staying with us this weekend."

"Can you call your parents then, please?" asked the female officer.

Mark slowly took his phone out of his pocket, his face filled with dread as he imagined what his mum was going to say about everything. Luke stood quietly, he looked sad and thought about how disappointed his mother and father would be in him. It had been almost a whole year since he had lost his temper like this, he thought he had it under control.

"She's not picking up," said Mark.

"What about your father," said the male officer.

"He doesn't live with us," said Mark hastily.

Mark looked down at the floor and then felt comforted by Mr Sunil's arm around his shoulders.

"His father passed away five years ago, it was a very bad traffic accident."

"We are sorry to hear that," said the officers. "Listen why don't you tell us what happened first and then we can see about getting in contact with someone."

The boys started telling the officers everything; from the football match; to the theft of the shopping bag; the taunts from the boys; and the fight that ensued. A tear dripped down Luke's cheek as he re-told and re-lived each physical moment.

"It sounds like you boys have been through a lot," said the female officer, "and whilst we understand you were only protecting your cousin, there is no excuse for hurting other people."

"Although I'm not sure *how* much you hurt them," said the male officer. "The woman outside described one of the boys as flying five feet in the air and I don't think that's possible. You don't have superhuman strength, do you?" he laughed.

Luke remained quiet and with his fingers nervously fumbled a pound coin he had in his pocket.

The policewoman spoke again, "Next time you have to walk away and get help boys, do you understand?"

Luke and Mark nodded.

"Fortunately the other boys fled the scene, so this is where the investigation stops but we have to tell a parent or guardian."

The boys nodded again.

"Would you mind trying your mum one more time for us please son?" asked the male officer.

Mark tried again but the phone just rang. After

a few more unsuccessful attempts the officers decided to drop both Luke and Mark back home. Mark was quiet on the ride back to the house and Luke noticed him shoot several worried glances over in his direction. As Luke looked out of the window at the cars passing by in the opposite direction, he replayed the events of the past hour. He was angry with himself, disappointed that he had not been able to control his rage, ashamed that he had used so much strength and worried that he might have seriously hurt one of the boys.

'What's wrong with me?' he thought, 'why am I like this?'

The police car came to a stop just outside Mark's house. It was five o'clock and Janice was waiting at the door, her phone in one hand and a panic-stricken look on her face.

"Good Lord, is everything okay officers, what is going on?" said Janice, as she rushed towards the car. "Mark I've just seen your missed calls, I'm so sorry, I went for a nap and slept for longer than I thought I would."

Janice noticed the redness and swelling on Mark's cheek as he, Luke and the officers stepped out of the car.

"Oh my gosh, what happened to you Mark?"

"It's okay mum," said Mark, as he walked past her and into the house, "we're okay."

"Oh Luke," said Janice quietly, fondling his hair as he too walked past her and into the house.

The boys watched from the upstairs window as the officers explained to Mark's mum what had happened that afternoon.

"Mark, Luke, come downstairs please, both of you."

Mark and Luke ventured slowly downstairs and hovered in the doorway of the kitchen. The officers had taken their leave and Janice was standing by the kitchen sink.

"The officers told me what happened boys, I hope you are both okay. I am so sorry you had to go through that."

Both Luke and Mark looked tired and deflated.

"Luke I heard you protected Mark, but next

time call for help. I don't care about the shopping, I just care that you are both safe and come back not hurt."

She reached into the freezer and took out some frozen peas, wrapped them in a tea towel and gently placed them on Mark's cheek.

"You both must be hungry, sit down and I will get your dinner ready."

The boys sat at the table quietly, Mark still hadn't looked at Luke properly since the park; and although Luke felt he knew why this was the case, it still hurt. They picked at their food and exchanged maybe five words between them throughout dinner. Janice observed them both and said, "I think an early night will do the both of you the world of good, and Luke, I won't tell your mum tonight because I don't want to worry her, but you do understand I will have to let her know in the morning."

"Yes Aunty J." Luke replied.

It was half past eight and the boys were upstairs in Mark's room, where they lay in their beds. Luke was sleeping on the makeshift pull-out bed, which was usually stored under

Mark's existing bed. He tossed and turned a few times before finding a comfortable position. It was dark in Mark's room and the only source of light came through a gap in the curtains where a fraction of the moon could be seen and cast a glimmer of light onto the wall. It was also quiet. Both boys laid with their backs to one another. This was far from one of Luke and Mark's usual sleepovers where Aunty J would have to come upstairs at least three times to tell them to be quiet and to go to sleep, as it was way past their bedtime.

'No,' Luke thought, 'this sucks, Mark won't even look at me, let alone talk to me, what was I supposed to do? I was only trying to protect him.'

Luke closed his eyes and decided to sleep, this way the morning would come by quicker and he wouldn't have to endure any more of Mark's awkward silent treatment. Just as Luke started to drift off he heard a familiar voice calling his name and his right shoulder being prodded.

"Luke, Luke."

Luke mumbled a very sleepy "what?" and

opened his eyes slowly.

It was Mark, looking down and staring right at him on the pull-out bed. From where his bed lay, Mark's face was slightly lit by the glow of the moon.

"Luke, what was that earlier? I've never seen you like that before."

Luke lay quiet and still in his bed whilst he decided what the best thing to say to Mark would be.

"I mean how did you manage to throw that guy so far?" continued Mark "and how on earth were you able to swing the other one round and round like that? They were at least twice our size."

Luke scratched his head.

"That was like something the Incredible Hulk would do," said Mark.

Luke slowly began to speak, "I guess I have always been really strong for as long as I can remember and, as you can see, it is not all good because with it comes the extreme rage issues."

Mark sat and listened, amazed at what he was hearing and curious as to why he had never noticed it before.

"That still doesn't explain how you are so strong though, that was superhuman strength."

Luke fidgeted a little under his covers, "If I tell you something do you promise not to tell anyone? Not even your mum."

Mark nodded eagerly, "I promise."

Luke decided to tell him everything, from the clinical trials where everything went wrong, according to his parents; to some of the past incidents where his rage had consumed him. Although he had promised his mum and dad that he would never share a word of this with anyone, he felt a weight lifted from every muscle in his body.

"Wow," said Mark slowly through a long drawn-out breath, "so you are like superhuman. How does it feel when the rage takes over?"

Luke laughed nervously, "I don't really know

how to describe it, it's like my eyes go blurry and I can only see the obstacle that is in front of me."

Mark listened intently, he was now sprawled on the edge of his bed, his head cupped in his hands underneath his chin, his eyes widening with every word spoken.

Luke continued, "All of my muscles tense up and it feels like someone else is controlling me and then it is like my body is moving on its own. And once I've calmed down my whole body feels really sore."

Mark could not believe what he was hearing.

"That sounds scary man and quite cool, do you think you'll be like this forever?"

A flicker of a grimace could be seen on Luke's face at hearing the word 'forever.'

"I hope not," he said.

Mark was quiet for a minute, deep in thought.

"Sorry I was so quiet on you earlier," he said, breaking the silence. "I think I was just in shock and I was going over everything in my head."

Luke smiled, he felt his usual self again.

"And don't worry I won't tell anyone, let's get some sleep now before we get into trouble for talking."

Luke and Mark grinned at each other tucked themselves back into bed and shortly after fell asleep.

The next morning they woke up to find pancakes and syrup awaiting them at the kitchen table.

"Something to brighten up your day," Janice told them as they sat down.

The pancakes certainly did put them in excellent moods and they were both back on top form, laughing away as usual and chatting about everything they could think of. They had just finished having breakfast when the doorbell rang, it was Luke's mum. Luke ran and gave her a long and tight hug.

"How have they been Janice?" asked Sylvia.

"Fine, fine" replied Sylvia, "Mark why don't

you go upstairs with Luke and help him pack his bag, I'm just going to fill your Aunty Sylvia in on a few things."

"Okay," chimed the boys and darted upstairs to pack.

The journey home was very tense and very long. Luke's mum proceeded to ask him what felt like a thousand questions about the incident, in between repeatedly asking him if he was okay and double-checking that he wasn't hurt.

"Luke I've messaged Dr Ashworth, I told him what happened and I thought it best to get you an emergency session."

Luke looked towards his mother.

"This way he can properly assess you, help to get you back on the right track, you know."

Luke felt glum, he couldn't help but feel that he had, in a really big way, disappointed his mother.

"Luke, I want you to know that you are not in trouble and you haven't disappointed me, I'm just worried that's all and I want what is best for you."

Luke nodded and was quiet for the rest of the journey.

As Sylvia drove, she reflected on when Luke was little and when play dates were nothing short of a nightmare for her. She remembered how she would often receive a phone call partway through, from the other child's parent, begging for her to pick Luke up. Usually, because he had really hurt their child, or because they were once again in the throes of calling the repair man round for a broken door. There was one phone call that Sylvia would never forget and it just so happened to come from the next-door neighbours. This incident in particular involved the dining room table and required the help of five grown men to dislodge it from the wall next to the stairwell.

"Mum are you okay?" asked Luke, breaking her train of thought.

"Yes dear, I'm okay – just a little tired, don't worry about me, "she replied.

Sylvia slipped back into her train of thought and also remembered how at one point, Grant had taken to going for long walks in the woods with Luke at least twice a week, directly after school; and how together just before Luke went to bed at night, they practiced deep breathing meditation. Despite their many efforts at the time, they had very little success as Luke struggled to keep his anger at bay; and found it increasingly harder to hide his abnormal strength. As each year passed, his parents worried that someone from the neighbourhood would talk or upload a video of Luke to SquareBase; and that they would one day open the front door to a camera crew who would undoubtedly turn Luke into 'The Highgate Freak Show.' Or worse yet, he would be taken away by scientists to be experimented on.

Once home, Luke was greeted by a massive hug from his father and a warming smile from a familiar face. It was Dr Ashworth, who stood waiting for him in his house. Once Luke had re-told the story to both his father and Dr Ashworth, for what felt like the hundredth time, Dr Ashworth asked if he could speak to Luke's parents alone. Luke obliged and went upstairs to his room to play. Luke hadn't heard anything from his parents or Dr Ashworth for what must have been at least twenty minutes, so he decided to venture downstairs. As he opened the front room door, he noticed that his mother's eyes were blotchy and red, just like they became after she had been crying. He also observed that his dad was pacing the room, just like he did when he was struggling to make a decision about something important.

"Ah Luke you're here, good timing," said Dr Ashworth.

"We've all been talking Luke and I want you to know that it was no easy decision for your mother and father."

"What wasn't?" interjected Luke.

"Well," started Dr Ashworth. "Due to yesterday's events and having considered all of our hard work and breakthroughs this previous year, I think it would be best if you attended Capel House Boarding School in Kent this September, instead of Highgate Hill."

"What, no!" exclaimed Luke. "That's not fair, all my friends will be going there."

Luke was fighting hard to hold back the tears he felt building.

"Now I know it doesn't sound like the most ideal situation at the moment and your parents have told me you had your heart set on Highgate Hill. Nevertheless, I feel there is still work to be done Luke. Also, I will be there, at Capel House, to keep an eye on you."

Dr Ashworth continued, "As you know, I am the lead psychologist at the school and I also live on-site."

Luke couldn't quite believe what he was being told, he didn't want to and quickly looked over to his mother for consolation.

"Mum, you don't agree with this do you?"

Sylvia burst into tears, "Oh Luke I'm so sorry but I do think this is best. This way Dr Ashworth can keep an eye on you and he's right, there are just too many triggers for you in London."

Luke started to cry now. His dad had stopped pacing.

"Dad," called out Luke, "What do you

think? Tell me this isn't true."

"I'm sorry son," said Grant as he tried to embrace him in a hug.

Luke pulled away and ran upstairs, back to his bedroom.

"Give him some time," said Dr Ashworth, "he will come around I'm sure."

"Thank you so much Dr Ashworth, I don't know what we would do without you."

"It's no problem Sylvia," he replied as he began to put on his coat and headed towards the door.

"I'll get the school application paperwork sent over to you tonight and I will fast-track Luke's admission, it shouldn't be a problem."

Grant closed the door behind Dr Ashworth as he walked down their garden path, he then turned to face Sylvia, gave her hug and said, "We are doing the right thing, I feel it in my bones. Everything is going to be okay."

Sylvia looked up at Grant from where her head rested on his chest and whispered softly, "I hope so."

It had been a long and hot summer in London and one of many ups and downs for Luke and his family. It was nearing the end of the six weeks holiday and was a little under two weeks before the new term was due to start. As scheduled, Luke had been receiving his weekly therapy sessions with Dr Ashworth. He was now in a place where he had accepted that he would be attending a different school from his friends and more importantly, that he would only really see his parents during the holidays. Luke had been measured for his school uniform which was due for collection the week before school started. Sylvia was relieved to have caught Luke smiling at himself in the shop mirror, whilst he tried it on and fastened the buttons on the blazer. He was even looking forward to joining the school's football team and playing in the games room in the evening. Dr Ashworth had shown Luke the school's prospectus and together had browsed through pictures of the grounds during their sessions. Luke felt the school had excellent sports facilities and decided that any school that had a games room was alright with him. During one of their sessions, Dr Ashworth had also told Luke that he would like him to meet someone very special whilst he was at Capel House Boarding School. Someone who had grown up with a handful of experiences not so unlike Luke's and that this person also happened to be his god-daughter and her name was Maya.

Five Worlds Apart Series

Join Luke on many other adventures.

Luke and his friends have been assigned the task of taking down Robert Mann, Robotics and Artificial Intelligence extraordinaire. As they make their way through a number of dangerous missions, they must also navigate and manage their feelings and friendships all whilst attending school during the day. The clock is ticking and they must prevent Robert Mann and his promise of a brighter future, for civilisation, from destroying the world as they know it.

Luke, Maya, Javier, Chris, and Amy possess a unique power that they must learn to harness and put to use for the greater good if they are to understand their worth and place in this world.

Printed in Great Britain
by Amazon